CONTENTS

BY TINA SHAW
ILLUSTRATED BY STEFAN MESSAM

THE GIRLFRIEND

PREDICT

What do you think this story could be about?
What helped you form your opinion?

PARADISO

Me and AJ have known each other forever. Since before the war started. That's, like, eight years ago. I remember 'cause we were both eight when it started.

At first it wasn't so bad. The rebels came, wanting to take over, except we Melanistas held them back. But things just got worse and worse. Both me and AJ, our parents vanished. I don't know where they went. I had a sister, too, but she's gone off somewhere. For the last six months I've been trying to find her.

Now AJ was saying he'd got a girlfriend.

"A what?" I spluttered when he first told me. But AJ was serious.

"COME ON, CLEM, DON'T GIVE ME GRIEF."

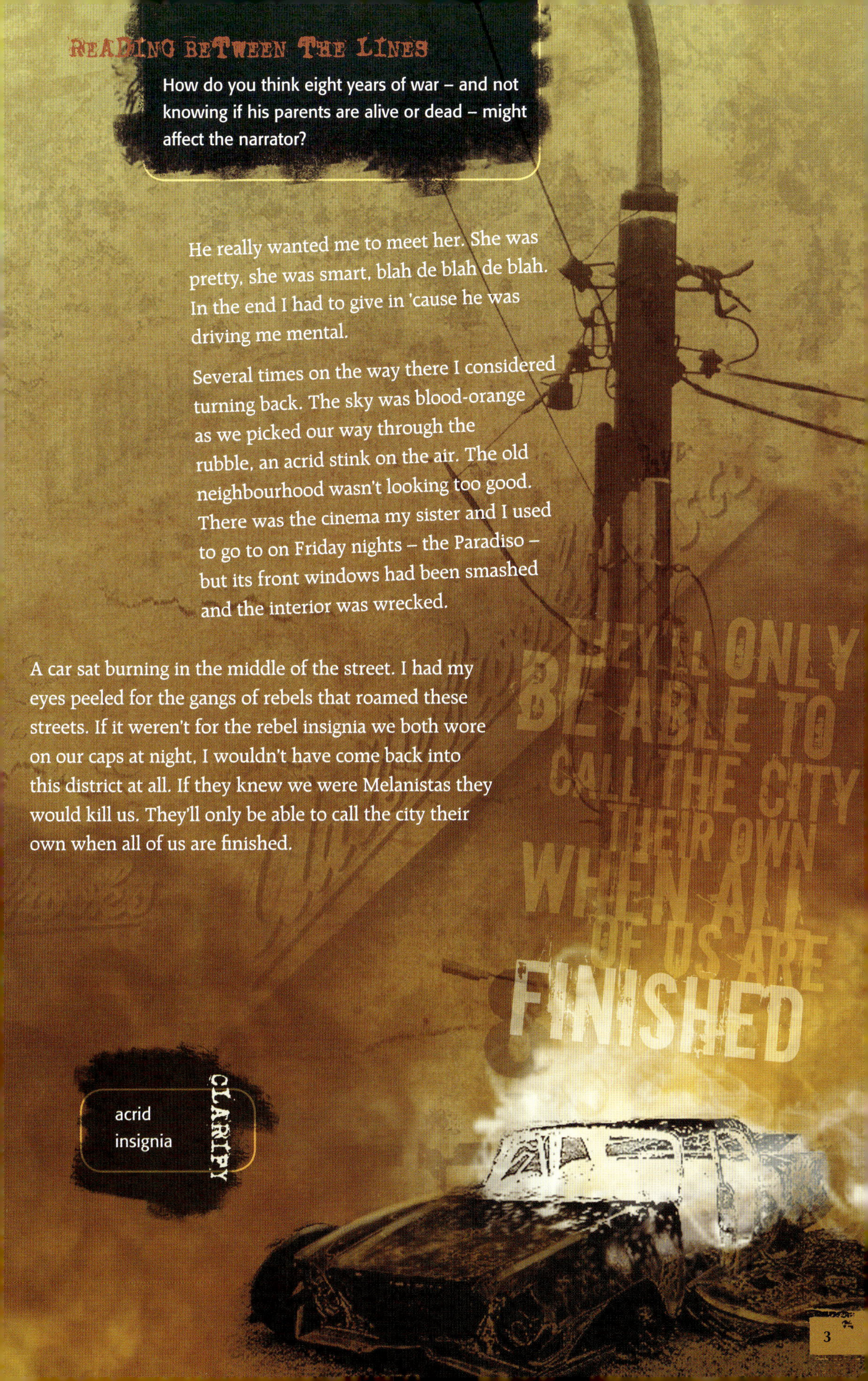

Reading Between The Lines

How do you think eight years of war – and not knowing if his parents are alive or dead – might affect the narrator?

He really wanted me to meet her. She was pretty, she was smart, blah de blah de blah. In the end I had to give in 'cause he was driving me mental.

Several times on the way there I considered turning back. The sky was blood-orange as we picked our way through the rubble, an acrid stink on the air. The old neighbourhood wasn't looking too good. There was the cinema my sister and I used to go to on Friday nights – the Paradiso – but its front windows had been smashed and the interior was wrecked.

A car sat burning in the middle of the street. I had my eyes peeled for the gangs of rebels that roamed these streets. If it weren't for the rebel insignia we both wore on our caps at night, I wouldn't have come back into this district at all. If they knew we were Melanistas they would kill us. They'll only be able to call the city their own when all of us are finished.

Clarify

acrid
insignia

"HEY," I hissed.

AJ paused, looking back. "WHAT?"

Flames flickered in his eyes. His cap pulled down low, he looked like a stranger, not somebody I'd known all my life. I was going to make some sarcastic remark about the random nature of life, but changed my mind. He might've hit me. "Nothing," I said.

A beat, no more, then he carried on, hunkered low, across the debris-strewn plaza and past the car. Black windows stared down at us from scorched and empty buildings. We stepped around a body on the pavement. The streets were suspiciously quiet.

CLARIFY

debris-strewn
plaza
complacent

VISUAL FEATURES

What effects do the visual images and design have on you? How do these features influence your response to the story so far?

"Hey," I called again.

"What?" he said over his shoulder, not stopping.

"How much longer?"

AJ didn't say anything. We'd been on the go for an hour, so it couldn't be too much further. I just hoped it'd be safe. It was hard to keep safe these days in the city. But it hadn't always been like this: there was a time when our city was a good place to live – there were trees, shops, schools, clubs; all the normal stuff you take for granted.

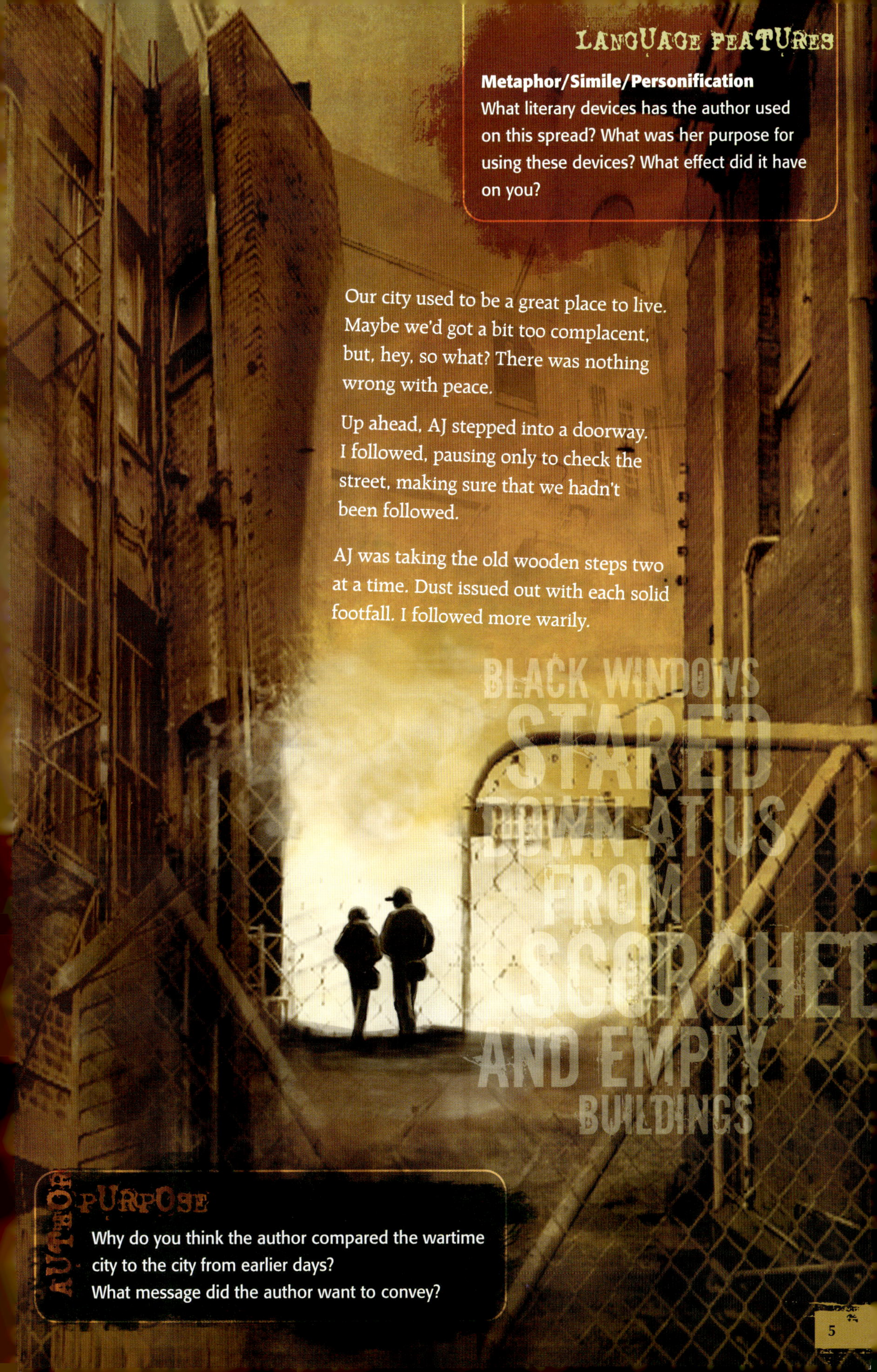

Language Features

Metaphor/Simile/Personification
What literary devices has the author used on this spread? What was her purpose for using these devices? What effect did it have on you?

Our city used to be a great place to live. Maybe we'd got a bit too complacent, but, hey, so what? There was nothing wrong with peace.

Up ahead, AJ stepped into a doorway. I followed, pausing only to check the street, making sure that we hadn't been followed.

AJ was taking the old wooden steps two at a time. Dust issued out with each solid footfall. I followed more warily.

BLACK WINDOWS STARED DOWN AT US FROM SCORCHED AND EMPTY BUILDINGS

Author Purpose

Why do you think the author compared the wartime city to the city from earlier days?
What message did the author want to convey?

THE MEETING

Upstairs, AJ tapped lightly on a closed door and listened. We shuffled for a few minutes. Maybe this had all been just a joke. Maybe he had talked to the girl, but she'd given him the flick. Anything was possible. From what he'd said, she was hot, the perfect chick. It was hard to believe. I could see he was having doubts, too, 'cause his ears had gone red. I almost felt sorry for the guy. From outside came the incessant cry of the sirens. Nothing unusual in that. It went on all night long.

Then the door swung open, and there she was, the most beautiful girl I'd ever seen. She was tall and thin, with spiky black hair and skin that gleamed dusky brown like the shell of a macadamia nut. I turned away as she and AJ smiled at each other, tongue-tied. It was pathetic. Eventually they remembered me, and AJ introduced us.

HER NAME WAS KOEVASI.

She shut the door behind her, a finger to her lips, and led us down the hall to another door. Inside there was an empty room with a dusty floor. This was obviously one of the buildings left behind when the Melanistas fled the district. Families would have lived here once. I didn't know what to do with my hands, so I shoved them in my jacket pockets.

There were some wooden boxes. Once this house would've had nice furniture. The rebels liked to throw nice chairs out of windows, then slit them open with their machetes. They did the same thing to people. AJ and the girl sat down on the boxes, but I stood over by the door, listening. I didn't like it there. The place made me nervous, like it was a trap. AJ and the girl were whispering to each other.

I cleared my throat, making a loud rasping noise, just to remind them they had company.

BEYOND THE TEXT

Can you relate to how the narrator is feeling as he waits to be introduced? What connections can you make?

LANGUAGE FEATURE

Analogy

What analogy did the author use here? How did it help your understanding? What did the author want to convey to the reader?

OPINION

Do you think the acts of war described in the text should be censored to protect the reader? Why/why not? What is your stance on the issue of censorship?

CHARACTER ANALYSIS

What inferences can you make about the narrator's feelings toward Koevasi and his reluctance to trust people?

AJ looked over. He was the old AJ, the way he used to look back in the good old days, his face plump with happiness, his eyes sliding from side to side like he didn't trust himself to speak. The girl looked at me, too. Her eyes were a shivery grey-green, like the inside of a porcelain vase.

"YOU ARE LOOKING FOR YOUR SISTER," she said.

"Maybe." I felt a plug of resentment that AJ had told her about that. It was private.

"PERHAPS I CAN HELP," she added.

"How's that?"

"I know some people. I could ask around."

That was the kind of thing we used to say to each other before the rebels came. Nobody said that kind of thing these days. You looked out for yourself. I gave a shrug, said nothing; I didn't want to commit myself to somebody I didn't trust. You had to be careful who you spoke to in the ci

"Who's in the next room?" I asked, ignoring AJ's frown.

The girl moved her head and her black hair gleamed in the light. "Just my family," she said.

I swallowed and looked at the floor. I wished I had family still.

CLARIFY

plug of resentment

OPINION
Do you think AJ should have passed on information about the narrator's missing sister to Koevasi? Why/why not?
PLUG
IT WAS
PRIVATE
PERSONAL RESPONSE
What feelings are evoked when the author writes about the narrator's wish that he still had family?

ANITA

For a while, me and my sister Anita had a squat in this same part of the city. When our parents were still around, it was green here – lots of trees, and we lived in a nice big house with a garden near the school. After our parents disappeared, we stayed on. But then one day the rebels grabbed our house – just took it while my sister and I were out, so we couldn't go back there. That's when we hunted for an abandoned apartment.

We had a routine: each day we'd go out to scavenge for food. Then we'd cook an evening meal on a little primus stove, which we'd eat together at the small table at the back of the apartment. AJ stayed with us, too,

HE HAD NOBODY ELSE LEFT.

There was a window that opened onto the courtyard below, so you couldn't be seen from the street. My sister had found some gauzy curtains that she put up. With the window open, the curtains shifted gently on the breeze. It was sort of like being back in peace.

CLARIFY

squat
primus stove

At night, from somewhere in the building, a guitar would pick out sad tunes. It made me wonder what had happened to our parents. Sometimes the music would make my sister cry, so I knew she was thinking about them, too.

PERSONAL RESPONSE

What feelings are evoked by the description of the adversities facing the characters in a war-torn city? How does this text influence your opinion of war?

What inference can you make about the disappearance of the narrator's sister?

SCAVENGING

But, after a while, Anita and I got on each other's nerves. She was older than me, my sister. She knew people. She was political, and we argued about that. Keep your head down, don't make trouble, that's what I said.

MY SISTER THOUGHT DIFFERENTLY.

She wanted to get a gun – always she was thinking about our parents. She was sure the rebels had killed them.

Maybe I was naïve, but I wasn't so sure. She wanted to join one of the Melanista cells and kill rebels. I wanted to stay out of the way, keep low. Why couldn't she be okay with that, too?

Then one day I came back from a day's scavenging and my sister was gone.

GONE

AN OASIS

We didn't stay long at the house. AJ murmured something to the girl, and we left the apartment. Clattering down the dusty old stairs, I was curious about where he'd met this Koevasi girl.

"I just bumped into her," he said, not wanting to talk about it.

"AND?"

He hunched his shoulders in his jacket. "There was an orange tree. We both found it at the same time." A secret remembering smile came to his lips. Those oranges – he brought two back for me. But he hadn't mentioned any girl.

VISUAL FEATURE

What effect does the illustration have on you?

Back out on the street (after checking in both directions before we stepped out onto the ashy pavement), he punched me in the arm, grinning hard and showing his broken front tooth. "Didn't I tell you?" he said. We were hurrying along, me trying to keep up with his jubilant pace. "She's great."

OPINION

Shoot first, ask questions later.

What is your opinion on this policy?

What do you think the opinion of the residents of the city and the soldiers might be?

Compare these three opinions.

"Sure, AJ," I agreed. But there was also something funny about her.

We ducked behind a rubbish skip as a tight bunch of Melanista soldiers jogged past. A night patrol. They'd probably shoot us if they saw the caps – even though we were on the same side. Shoot first, ask questions later.

SHOOT FIRST, ASK QUESTIONS LATER

"And she's going to find out about your sister," said AJ, as if this girl was the heroine of the universe.

"Uh-ha," I muttered, pulling my cap low.

CLARIFY

jubilant

His happiness was kind of repulsive to me. It made me want to etch lines into my arm with the point of a very sharp knife. It reminded me of a life we'd all once had, which we wouldn't see again. It reminded me that I'd once been a different kind of person.

Just last night, for instance, I had come across a man who was lying bleeding on the street, a man who was still alive, a man who looked up at me with beseeching eyes.

In the old days, I would've got him to a hospital. (We still had a hospital here in the city, though there was no guarantee that they could help you, supplies being so short, ditto doctors.) Instead, I crouched down by his side, his eyes on me the whole time, and slipped the watch off his broken wrist.

CHARACTER ANALYSIS

How do you think the war has affected the narrator?

The Narrator Before the War

The Narrator in Wartime

READING BETWEEN THE LINES

Why has the author told us that the narrator stole a watch off a bleeding man in the street? Is there an underlying message here? What is your opinion?

CLARIFY

beseeching
ditto

AJ and I went back to our cubbyhole in the old warehouse. In through the sack curtain at the back of the loading bay, along the low, narrow corridors – where once small carts would have delivered goods – down the trapdoor in the floor, along another corridor, then we were home. AJ lit a candle, and I set about heating some water on the primus. We'd got hold of some coffee, which we'd make up in tiny amounts, taking worshipful sips from the metal cup.

SYMBOLISM

Why do you think the illustrator has used a bird and island scenes in the illustration on page 17? What do these images symbolise to you?

"Koevasi talks about the war like it's only a short-term thing," AJ was saying, as if we'd never stopped talking about the girl. "She reckons it can't last, that things'll get better…"

AJ, squatting on the floor, eyes gleaming in the candlelight, was obviously still in a state of entrancement. He lifted the cup thoughtfully to his lips, took a sip, then handed it across to me. "Meanwhile, she's trying to get people out of the city," he said.

"SHE'S OFFERED TO GET US OUT."

I looked at the oily blackness of the coffee in the mug.

"She's got this place, Clem, where it's safe. This place she can take us to. It sounds awesome."

There was something about all this I didn't like. And AJ sounded delusional. I eyed him curiously, waiting to see what would come next. He huffed out a sigh, and settled into his coat like a chicken ruffling its feathers.

"Don't you wish you could get out of the city?" he said. "I mean, you're still looking for your sister, I know that. But, once you find her, we could all go to this place with Koevasi and her family…"

His eyes glazed over like he was picturing some place with palm trees and clean water, some kind of pretty oasis a long way away from the war.

PERSONAL RESPONSE

Do you think AJ has been led into believing in something that is too good to be true? What connections can you make to this?

"Me, I'd really like to go to a place like that." He glanced up, suddenly shy. "You gonna come, too, Clem?"

I looked at the floor. Sometimes I dreamed about a place that was green and quiet, the way the city used to be – safe. A place where my sister and I would be walking barefoot through soft grass. A warm breeze would brush the hem of her dress against her bare knees. A bird would be singing in the blue sky.

AJ WAS WAITING FOR ME TO SAY SOMETHING.

I stood up, handing him the mug. "You finish the coffee," I said.

CLARIFY

cubbyhole
entrancement
delusional
oasis

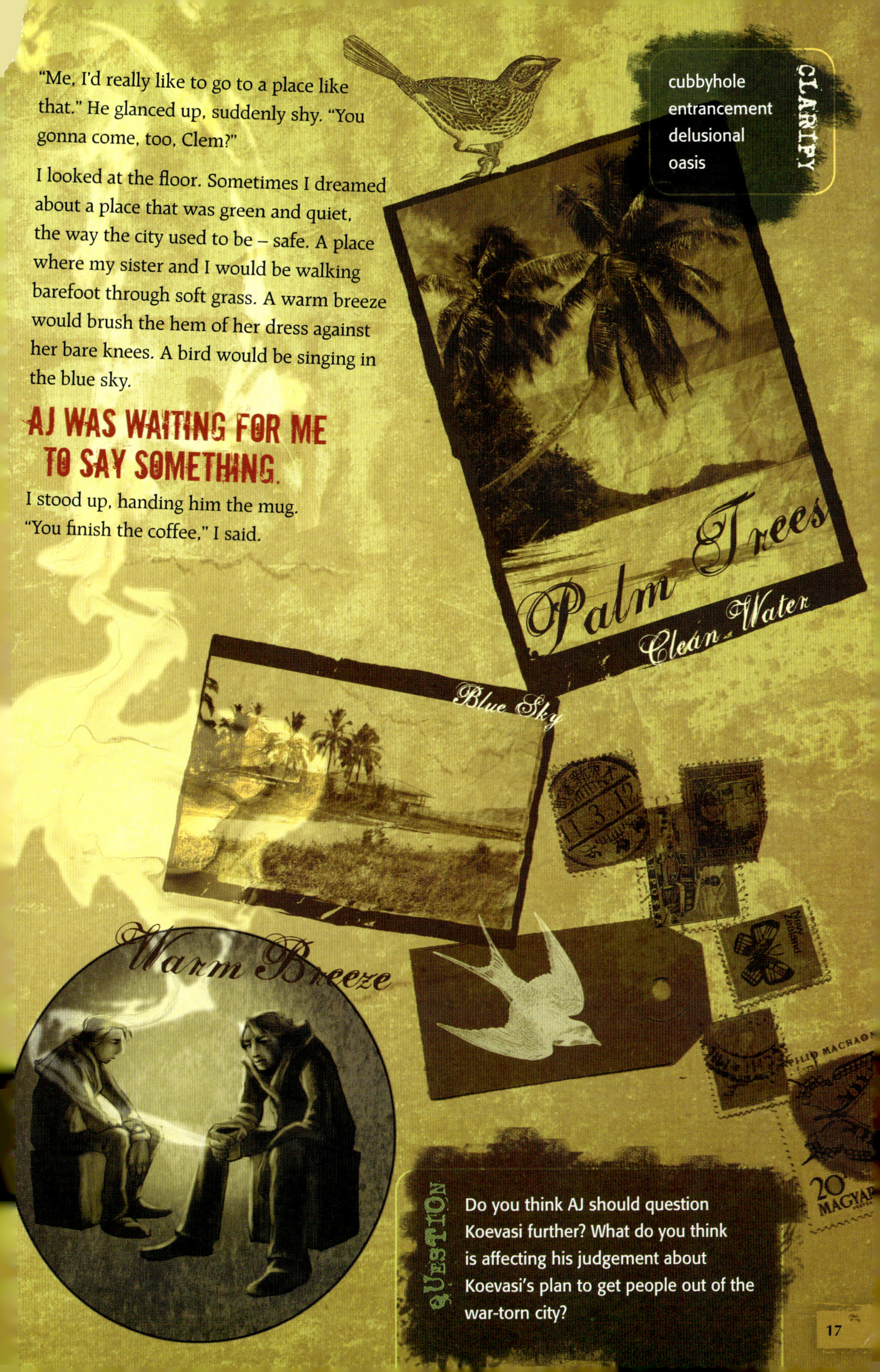

QUESTION

Do you think AJ should question Koevasi further? What do you think is affecting his judgement about Koevasi's plan to get people out of the war-torn city?

THE BETRAYAL

As AJ snored through the darkest hours, I padded out into the deserted streets and made my way back across the city to Koevasi's apartment. But this time I didn't go through the door on the street. I went around to the rear entrance instead.

CLARIFY
illumination

A skinny cat flashed past me, across the dirty inner courtyard. There was no other sign of life. Not even a light in one of the rooms, though I suspected many people lived in this building. I took off my boots, tied the laces together and hung them around my neck. Then I started silently up the metal fire escape that led to the girl's apartment.

A window opened onto the fire escape. There were blinds, but they were crooked and broken, so I could see through the gaps. Inside was the room with the boxes where we had sat. The sky, which was lit up nightly by fires, cast a dim illumination into the room.

No sign of Koevasi. **MAYBE SHE WAS IN THE OTHER ROOM.**

SUSPECTED

BIAS

Do you think the narrator's mistrust of Koevasi reflects a personal bias? Why/why not?

I made myself comfortable on the metal ledge. There was something about the eerie nature of the room that made me want to wait, to watch. It was like sitting in a theatre and looking at the stage before the actors came out. Maybe it was my imagination – or maybe it was just that I didn't want AJ to go away to some lovely place and leave me behind in the city, relentlessly looking for my sister, who might not even still be alive – but I was prepared to wait for as long as it took.

So I waited while the skinny cat crept back into the yard and started scouting through the rubbish littering the ground. I waited while a shadowy figure entered the other side of the building, and a candle was lit in one of the lower rooms. I waited while gunfire sounded in a distant part of the city, and the sky lightened through several shades of black to deep blue.

I WAITED...

PREPARED TO WAIT FOR AS LONG AS IT TOOK

SETTING

How effectively have the author, illustrator and designer developed the mood and atmosphere of the setting? Have images of war from newspapers and TV helped you determine the credibility of the setting? Why/why not?

It got hard to keep my eyes open. Maybe I dozed off. But then the door to the room opened. I crouched lower on the fire escape. There were three people, one of them carrying a lantern. All of them wore the insignia of the rebels and all of them carried guns slung over their shoulders.

They pulled up the boxes and sat down, talking quietly. Too quietly for me to hear. It was obviously one of the rebel cells. A man with curly black hair was gesturing with his hands, as if telling a story. A woman held out a map, and they all pored over it. And the girl – AJ's girlfriend – poked her finger at the map.

AJ! I had to get back, had to warn him. The three kept talking for a while longer, then the woman folded up the map. They left the room as the sky was turning to mauve – another few minutes and they would've seen me at the window – and I took the chance to take off down the fire escape.

PLOT

What do you think will happen in the storyline now?

PREDICT
What significance will the news of Koevasi's connection to the rebels have for AJ? How do you think he will feel about Clem's spying?

TRUE FRIENDS

"Look, you've got to listen to me!"

I grabbed AJ's shoulders, aware that I was babbling like a crazy guy. He listened coolly as I told him what I'd seen, then just as coolly he left the room, grabbing his jacket on the way out.

"Hey!" I cried, hurrying after him. In one of the dim warehouse corridors, I caught a handful of his jacket. He spun round and took a swing at me.

"Hey," I cried, hurt now – not by the swing, which I'd adroitly ducked, but because AJ had never tried to hit me before. He was already hurrying on, me tagging along behind.

"I'm not making this up!" I shouted at his back.

BEYOND THE TEXT

Do you think AJ gave his friend a fair chance to speak up about the events he saw from the fire escape? Why/why not? What connections can you make to this?

He turned, and I thought he was going to try hitting me again. But there were tears in his eyes. "The one good thing," he spluttered. "The one good thing that happens to me, and you want to wreck it."

I let him go, listening as he made his way out of the building. I could have said it again – she's one of the rebels – but even to my own ears it sounded false, envious.

INFERENCE

What inferences can you draw from the fact that the narrator never repeats his accusation about Koevasi and her connection to the rebels?

Despite all that, I followed him anyway, at a distance, back through the streets to Koevasi's apartment, where I watched the doorway swallow him. Was I brave enough to follow him inside? I shuffled outside on the pavement, in a nervous fug. What if they shot him? Surely it was a trap. But then I heard the rumble of a tank – the street wasn't any place to be hanging about – and made a dash for the doorway.

LANGUAGE FEATURES

Metaphor/Simile/Personification

What literary devices has the author used here?
How did it help your understanding?

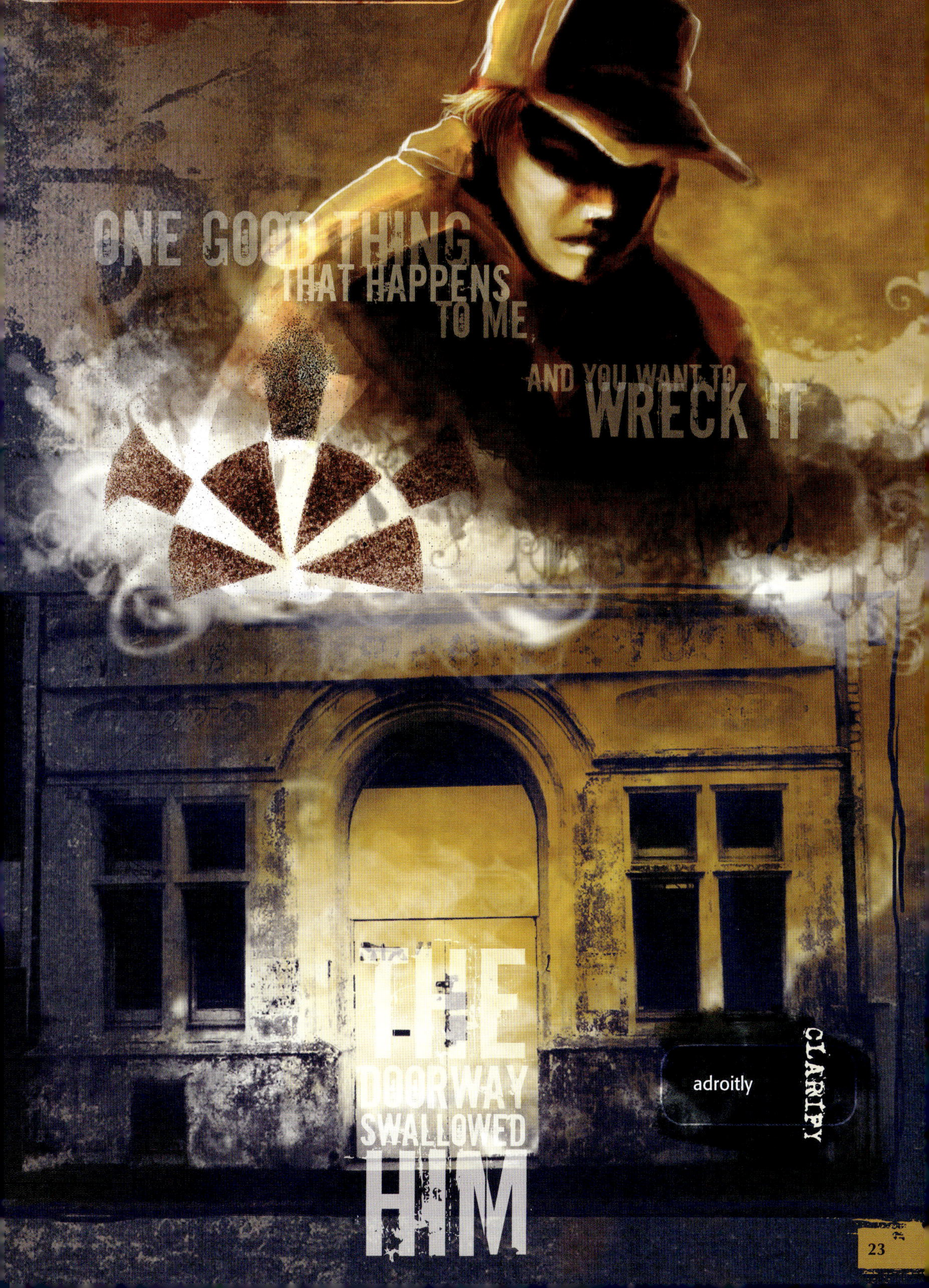

ONE GOOD THING THAT HAPPENS TO ME, AND YOU WANT TO WRECK IT

THE DOORWAY SWALLOWED HIM

CLARIFY

adroitly

At the top of the stairs, the apartment door was ajar. A sound of weeping was coming from within. I pushed the door open wider and peered inside. AJ was sitting beside Koevasi, his head in his hands. It was him that was weeping. Koevasi looked straight at me, her glossy eyes giving nothing away.

"HERE IS YOUR FRIEND," she told AJ.

With a swipe at his face, he came to the door and faced me. Koevasi stood behind him, like a true friend. I felt a stab of jealousy. Maybe AJ had found the real thing after all. Then again, maybe the war had unhinged his mind.

He came over and pushed me back out the door, shutting it behind him. So it was over, I was thinking with relief. AJ had broken up with the girl, and we could carry on like we always had, just him and me. We could try and forget about the danger he'd been in, maybe we'd even be able to laugh about it one day.

"I'm going with them – today. You'll have to make your own way now," said AJ. He looked older and wiser than I'd ever seen him before. He sniffed and rubbed his sleeve across his nose. "We're leaving the city today," he added.

That was when my sight went dark and I took a blind swing at him. He didn't duck or anything, but stood there and took it as my fist pounded into his cheek. His head jerked back and he gave a quiet splutter.

INFERENCE

What inferences can you make about why AJ was weeping, yet still wants to leave the city with Koevasi?

PREDICT

What effect will AJ's leaving have on the narrator?

YOU'LL HAVE TO MAKE YOUR OWN WAY NOW

AUTHOR PURPOSE

Why do you think the author wrote this story? What messages does she want to convey to the reader?

"I didn't expect you to understand," he said.

"And I don't," I said bitterly, already turning away and starting down the steps. It felt like all of our history had been cancelled out in a split second.

"HEY," he called.

AJ stood at the top of the stairs, looking down at me with a thin smile, his eye already starting to swell and colour. He held out a business card. "Koevasi told me to give you this." I snatched it out of his hand. There was one word printed on purple stock: Underground. It was a club on the other side of town. "She said you might find your sister there."

Anita? I looked up, meeting his eye. A blade of hope cut through me. I pictured going down into this club below the street, pushing my way through a crowd of brave souls, and finding my sister.

AJ held out his hand.

I couldn't ever stay mad at AJ for long. I reached up and we shook.

"We're heading north," he said. "Come find us some day."

I nodded, turning away. Even some of the rebels must get sick of the war. But, even if I did find my sister, it was unlikely I'd ever leave the city.

IT WAS WHERE I BELONGED.

PERSONAL RESPONSE

"It felt like all of our history had been cancelled out in a split second." What feelings are evoked by this text?

Reading Between the Lines

What is the significance of the card that may help the narrator find his sister? What does this symbolise for the narrator?

Question Generate

What questions could be asked about this text?

THINK ABOUT THE TEXT

MAKING CONNECTIONS

What connections can you make to the characters, plot, setting and themes of **KOEVASI?**

TEXT TO SELF

Being jealous

Facing danger

Living with grief and emotional turmoil

Facing change beyond your control

Being desensitised

Mistrusting people

Feeling angry and abandoned

Facing adversity

Being afraid

TEXT TO TEXT/MEDIA

Talk about texts/media you have read, listened to or seen that have similar themes and compare the treatment of theme and the differing author styles.

TEXT TO WORLD

Talk about situations in the world that might connect to elements in the story.

PLANNING A CONTEMPORARY FICTION

Contemporary fiction incorporates many different genres, such as mystery, science fiction, adventure, narrative, recount...

1 Think about what defines contemporary fiction

Contemporary fiction connects the reader with the complex situations and events of contemporary society. It incorporates themes and contexts that are seen as:

- a reflection of the past
- a mirror of the present
- an indicator of the future.

2 Think about the plot

Decide on a plot that has an introduction, problems and a solution, and write them in the order of sequence.

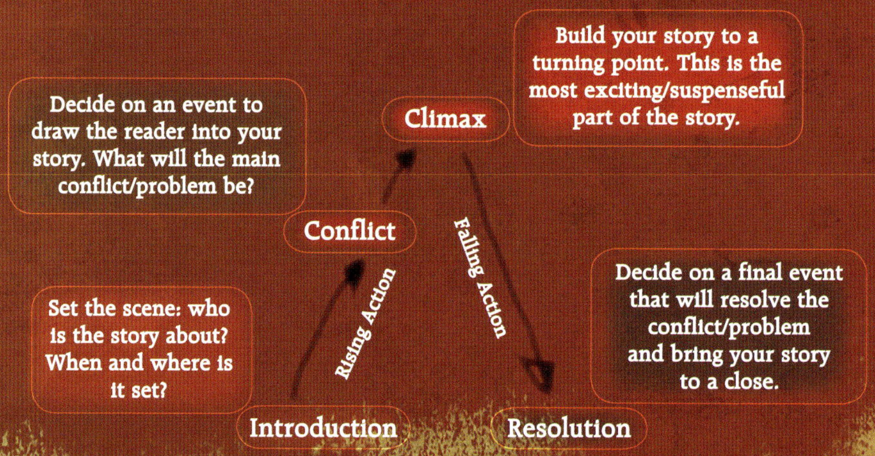

Build your story to a turning point. This is the most exciting/suspenseful part of the story.

Climax

Decide on an event to draw the reader into your story. What will the main conflict/problem be?

Conflict

Falling Action

Decide on a final event that will resolve the conflict/problem and bring your story to a close.

Set the scene: who is the story about? When and where is it set?

Rising Action

Introduction

Resolution

Think about the sequence of events and how to present them using contemporary fiction devices, such as *flashback* and *foreshadowing*.

Flashback = showing part of the storyline out of sequence.
Foreshadowing = suggesting or indicating events before they happen.

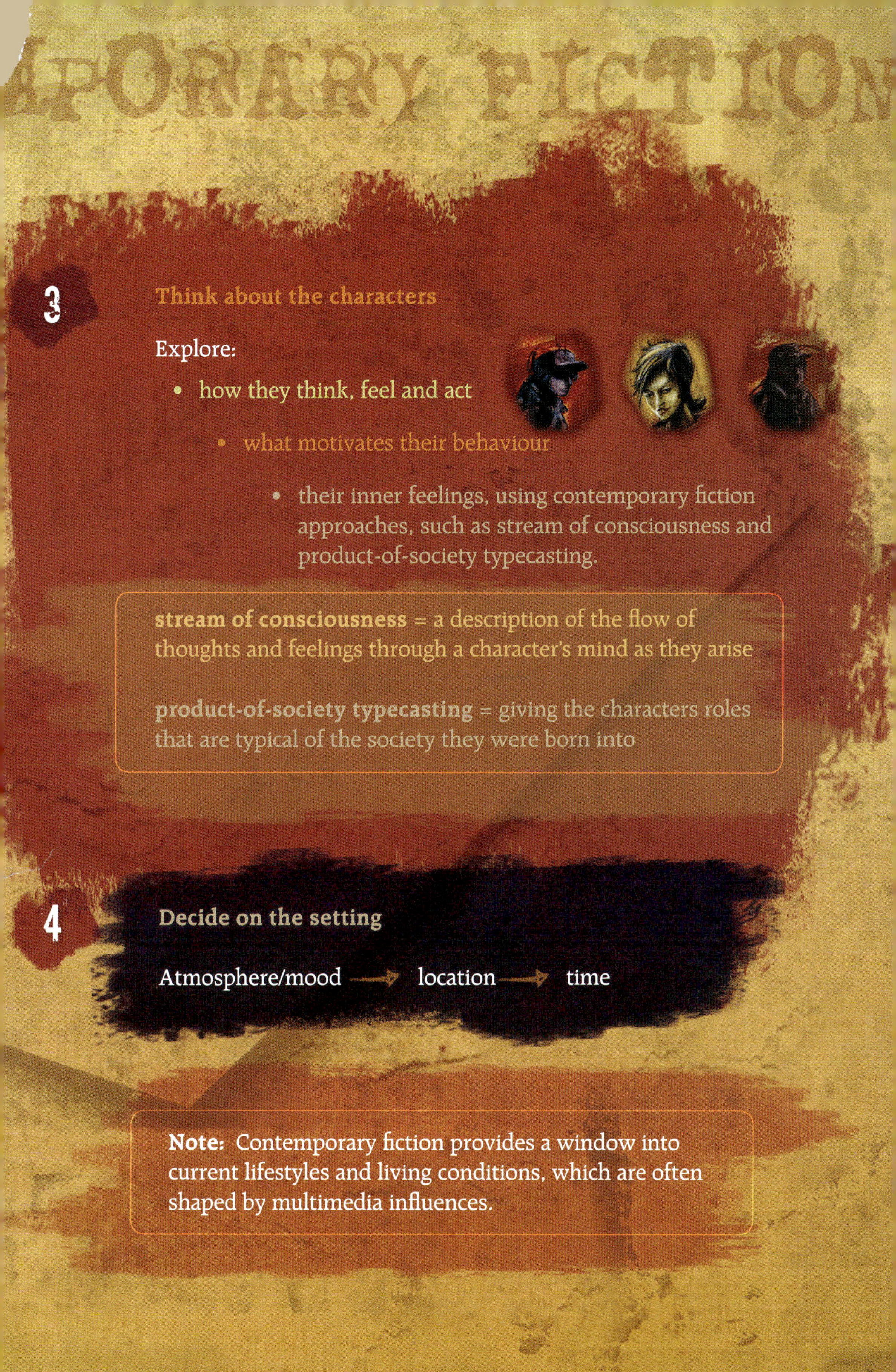

3 Think about the characters

Explore:

- how they think, feel and act
- what motivates their behaviour
- their inner feelings, using contemporary fiction approaches, such as stream of consciousness and product-of-society typecasting.

stream of consciousness = a description of the flow of thoughts and feelings through a character's mind as they arise

product-of-society typecasting = giving the characters roles that are typical of the society they were born into

4 Decide on the setting

Atmosphere/mood → location → time

Note: Contemporary fiction provides a window into current lifestyles and living conditions, which are often shaped by multimedia influences.

WRITING A CONTEMPORARY FICTION

Have you . . .

- Made links to the society and events of your period?
- Identified with recurrent contemporary themes?
- Maintained a fast pace of action?
- Grabbed the readers' attention and dragged them from the first page to the final page?
- Been true to the context of your time frame?
- Provided a window on the past or present or future?
- Explored contemporary values and beliefs?
- Developed characters that will stand up to in-depth analysis?

. . .don't forget to revisit your writing.

Do you need to change, add or delete anything to improve your story?